JON AGEE
MY RHINOCEROS

Scallywag Press Ltd
LONDON

First published in Great Britain in 2022 by Scallywag Press Ltd,
10 Sutherland Row, London SW1V 4JT

Originally published in the USA by Michael De Capua Books/Scholastic

The rights of Jon Agee to be identified as the author and illustrator of this
work have been asserted by him in accordance with the Copyright, Design
and Patents Act, 1988

Printed on FSC paper in China by Toppan Leefung

001

British Library Cataloguing in Publication
Data available

ISBN 978-1-912650-99-6

When I bought my rhinoceros, I didn't really know what I was getting into.

He was a nice animal. Quiet, shy.
He stayed in the garden. Kept to himself.

I called a rhinoceros expert.
"Does he pull on his leash?" she asked.
"No," I said.
"Does he attack other rhinoceroses?"
"No," I said.
"Does he poo on the rug?"
"No!" I said.

"So what's the problem?"

"He doesn't do *anything*," I said.

"Actually," she said, "rhinoceroses only do two things. Pop balloons and poke holes in kites."

I couldn't believe it. Pop balloons and poke holes in kites?! How pathetic.

And then I thought: What if we went to the park and there was a man selling balloons?

Luckily, nothing happened.

But what if somebody was flying a kite?

Lots of kids were flying kites.
But nothing happened.
My rhinoceros didn't pop balloons!
He didn't even poke holes in kites!

I began to wonder about my rhinoceros.
Maybe he was a clunker. Maybe I should have
bought a hippopotamus instead.

On the way home from the park, I saw a robbery! One of the robbers was getting away in a balloon, the other was escaping in a kite.

The robber in the balloon was taunting the crowd.

I looked at my rhinoceros and pointed to the balloon. "Pop!" I said.

To my surprise, my rhinoceros leapt into the air.
He swooped at the balloon with his horn.
POP! went the balloon and down fell the robber.

I looked up at my rhinoceros and pointed to the
robber in the kite. "Poke a hole!" I yelled.

My rhinoceros swooped over and poked a big hole in the kite.

Down fell the robber.

Everybody was amazed by my rhinoceros.

The police chief raced up to me. "Is this your rhinoceros?"

"Yes," I said.

"Well, you've got a really special one. He can pop balloons and poke holes in kites!"

"I know," I said. "And guess what else?"

"He can fly, too!"

I don't think I'll buy a hippopotamus.